In the face of extremes that can pull us under—illness, addiction, loss—Julie LeMay's "rough heart" perseveres in this powerful collection by "taking care of the next thing in front" of her. Set mainly in harsh, beautiful Alaska, these tight yet rich and layered poems offer us both the authority of experience and the authority of place. LeMay carries with her the knowledge of a survivor who has learned what she can carry forward and what she must leave behind. She teaches us that sweetness is always bitt~~~
always hard-won. None of us knows what l
the uncertain and tenuous future, these ir
thing to hold onto.

—JIM DANIELS, author of *Birth Marks, Eig*

Julie LeMay's poems in *The Echo of Ice Letting Go* pull us close, ask us to embrace ecstasy, faith, and joy in the face of the *world's rough heart*. These poems honor the majesty of the mountains and skies of Alaska and Tibet, while at the same time acknowledging the difficulty we encounter in these bodies and here on this ground. LeMay's work gives sustenance, and *the faith of fast small wings;* we get *the whole/land in every mouthful:/taste willow bud, /muskeg, winter sun.* The music and clarity of image in these poems pull us toward something larger within, as well as outside of ourselves. This book is a pleasure to read; there's a generous, honest, courageous spirit at work here, a poet who knows how to praise this world in all its raggedness, beauty, and grief. This is a transformative, magical collection of poems, something readers will come back to over and over.

—CAROL POTTER, author of *Some Slow Bees,* winner of the 2014 Field Poetry Prize from Oberlin College Press.

Even when Julie LeMay is describing nature and Alaska—a stunned bird, a trapped moth, an ice lake—she is more than a poet of place. This gentle meal of resiliency, community, illness, and transcendence offers "the whole/ land in every mouthful". These poems that don't look away from death and other unimaginables (spousal violence, children's pain, illness and loss), confront the gaze of each unbearable life transition calmly, accommodating, and then accommodating further, moving each word out with a map-maker's commitment to get the knowable down. LeMay's poems poise there on the edge of each mystery, admiring: "In my sky there is no /god. But even in this damp cold/I could kneel..."

—JENNY FACTOR, author of *Unraveling at the Name*

What does a body know, or better yet, what does the body have the capacity to know? In Julie Hungiville LeMay's debut book, *The Echo of Ice Letting Go,* this question of the body hums throughout from the very first poem. From the onset, we are confronted with the delicate nature of the body's desire, "Maybe/ love is a con/ man's con, faith/ cobbled in misery." Is love fleeting or here for only tricks and twisting jabs? From the onset, LeMay prepares us for the encounter of "Life" being "pregnant/ with death" a motif the rest of the poems in her book wrestle with or celebrate. What LeMay offers are rich and personal histories as we excavate through Alaska or Tibet or the many beautiful land/sky-scapes she brings us to. And so, it is the journey that the body knows, and we move with this body of work with a Marlboro in hand, floating down a river at night or in a big truck rolling through a canyon.

To be honest, it took me awhile to read *Echo of Ice Letting Go,* mostly because these poems are like looking out at the sky at daybreak or dusk: your smallness amidst all the vastness and expanse. I would read three or four of the poems, then I had to stop just to breathe a bit before I read on some more. I discovered that these poems are vespers reminiscent of Mary Oliver's quiet observance— prayers or prayer time best linked to the heart. LeMay's work grounds us the way a kiss from our children keeps us; or the way a dead friend pleasantly haunts our memory; or the way nature envelopes us "*back/ into the immeasurable blue.*" Echo of Ice Letting Go is a wonderfully bountiful debut because each poem does what good poems should: appreciate and remind us to simply "Look:/ this day", our bodies are alive and present.

—F. DOUGLAS BROWN is the author of *Zero to Three* (University of Georgia Press 2014), recipient of the 2013 Cave Canem Poetry Prize

The Echo of Ice Letting Go

THE ECHO OF
ICE LETTING GO

JULIE HUNGIVILLE LEMAY

UNIVERSITY OF ALASKA PRESS

FAIRBANKS

Text © 2017
University of Alaska Press

Published by
University of Alaska Press
P.O. Box 756240
Fairbanks, AK 99775-6240

Cover and interior design by Kristina Kachele Design, llc.
Cover image: "Sockeye Run" by Ian Grant, 2016 (*www.iangrantart.com*).
Author photo by Heidi Burtch/Relic Photographic

Library of Congress Cataloging-in-Publication Data
Names: LeMay, Julie Hungiville, 1954author.
Title: The echo of ice letting go / Julie Hungiville LeMay.
Description: Fairbanks, Alaska : University of Alaska Press, 2017. | Includes
bibliographical references.
Identifiers: LCCN 2016025502 (print) | LCCN 2016033089 (ebook) | ISBN
9781602233119 (pbk. : alk. paper) | ISBN 9781602233126 ()
Classification: LCC PS3612.E4534 A6 2017 (print) | LCC PS3612.E4534 (ebook) |
DDC 811/.6dc23
LC record available at https://lccn.loc.gov/2016025502

For Eowyn and Forrest

CONTENTS

I

TOSCA LIVED A GOOD LIFE

Tosca on her knees sings
    of her good life,
    of her great love, why
    it should exempt her

from suffering. Maybe
    love is just a con
    man's con, faith
    cobbled with misery.

Life is pregnant
    with death, a prayer
    dead on the altar, just
    sad fish, sad fish.

The Madonna in her mantle
    sings a death song to the sky
    and is still beautiful. I ride
    with sadness. I am ripe with sorrow.

I am perched, I am hanging, Sir.
What will this seat cost me?

IN THE BELLY OF THE WHALE

We pray in the belly of a whale,
low rafters like ribs enclose us.
Bob Dylan croaks *forever young*
and Joni and I wish we had a river
to skate away on. I am wholly
smothered by darkness and winter-
wet wool. This is my story:
chairs groan under the weight
of the living. My daughter,
eight months pregnant, delivers
the eulogy. In the mourning

our songs drift away. No light
shines because an elegy
for a young mother drowns
the sky. This is not my
story but ten years from now
I will remember this day
and poetry will fail
me. The hymnal slams itself shut
and I stumble through another tune.
The pale sun never rises, only trolls
the cold horizon for echoes of our songs.

A NEW TOOLBOX

Two years ago, living on
the streets—at some point even cheap
hotels will kick out a young guy with cash
when windows get sealed with worn
blankets, yesterday's papers, and stolen

duct tape—he told me:
Mom, my old babysitter is in the Hell's
Angels. She's No-Name now.
They took some guys out
KGB Road. You know what that means.

I don't. But I've learned not
to ask. Meth madness
makes me miss
his heroin-quiet thievery. Except for
those near-fatal overdoses.

He texted me today. Methadone
makes his life easier, even if it's not
prescribed. He's three weeks into
his first job in three years. *I just got made*
apprentice. Getting paid to learn.

Once he asked me, *Did you know
the universe is 13 billion years old?*
Today he told me
he's just taking care
of the next thing in front of him.

Me too.

RECENT BLOOD TESTS ARE INDICATIVE OF A CANCER RECURRENCE

All summer I watched the yellow joy
of warblers flick and fidget, fly skyward,
dive earthward. It's autumn now
and they've flown home.
Only cottonwood leaves flutter yellow,

then die to the earth, anneal
to soil. In my sky there is no
god. But even in this damp cold
I could kneel to the sacrifice of leaves,
to the faith of fast small wings.

WHAT I LOST THAT DAY
IN GIFFORD, PENNSYLVANIA

The bees grumbled, an angry
mob conspiring trouble. Late
summer 1966 and twelve years
old, what did I know? Those yellow-
jackets rumbled an omen of murder
in Memphis, beatings in Chicago.
My childhood would soon disappear
like cotton-candy melts, stales
on a rough tongue. The bees didn't

know, they only waited for their own
death. Grandfather Mike stomped
the long wood walkway in heavy boots,
giant gloves and beekeeper's
veil, his head huge and disfigured.
They say it isn't true, that he wore
nothing monstrous but I remember
his face. The bees muttered,
talked about Mike, how he shouted *Jesus*

Christ, Mabel when mashed
potatoes grew cold or his water
in its glass tumbler stood lukewarm.
Grandmother Mabel's hands flew to fix
all errors, the uneasy apron of sorrow
tied tight around her waist. She avoided
the front door where bees circled
their prey. The bees refused to negotiate
a surrender so Mike threatened

with fist, curse, then insecticide.
I waited off the walkway on sweet
summer grass and watched my
grandfather battle the hive.
They confer about their fate,
but no bees will fly into tomorrow.
Mabel left by the back door,
Mike adjusted his thick gloves,
and day crept towards heavy night.

NO MORE WORDS

The poetry ended like a spent log of fuel.
I could not see, but a singe
of flame remained. No,

> this is an ache, an errant pain
> of dead ones who call me *lamb*.

My eyes examine the sky
and glorify fire and peril.
My own house

> dissolves. Water everywhere
> and writing the last vague line.

The sky disintegrates
and slowly the planets.

> They were somber
> sober performers
> for flesh, for fire, for flowers.

WHAT MEANING

Prayer repeats only desperate echoes

of childhood faith: unreachable patriarch,

impossibly-virgin mother. Fluffs of god-clouds

that polish sapphire skies are not revealed

by meditation. Instead sleepless

nights arrive in a meteor shower of words

that fall through my mind in varied voices:

I wouldn't do that if I were you . . . Looks

like snow . . . tomorrow, tomorrow. At least

near the creek-bed, solid stones stub and stumble

my booted feet, the glacier breathes cold on my tired

face. Scrub cottonwood emits a bell-like *ting*

as each raindrop bounces off a leaf, tumbles

downward onto rock. On the hillside, scattered

erratics erect as sentinels have watched

these waters for more than a thousand thousand

years. Walking downhill, I bow my head

against the increasing damp. Even

a light rain will accumulate.

NOT A FAIRY-TALE ENDING

for Gary

His voice and hands were magic
when he cradled the borrowed Gibson
and sat cross-legged and lanky on the wooden
floor of the old Boulder rental. His lit
Marlboro cigarette, poised upright
between the guitar's string and tuning peg,
rolled out wisps of smoke. His hair

was a lion's dirty halo and with a frog-prince
face, it seemed that his transformation
was never completed. She was eighteen
and believed their child
within her was a sealed promise
for a perfect future. But later,

he washed dishes, drove a truck,
ended up in the coal mine, and drank
Budweiser at their wooden kitchen table
after his graveyard shift, smoked
a pack-and-a-half a day, never
picked up the guitar. In mid-winter

1976, on the way to the laundromat
in their '69 Volkswagen, she took off
her silver wedding band, put it
in the glove box. It rolled around
for weeks until he found it with the empty
gum wrappers, bits of tobacco,
loose change, and lint. He left her

a widow at twenty-two.
When the county sheriff phoned
she only heard *overdose*. It was June
before she held the official
cause of death unknown typed
on a pale brown form.

DEAR BECKY

I just found your note to me, dated
in 1979, the day after your son was born,
my son still not born then, not even
conceived. The year before, we splashed
in hot springs along the highway
between Glenwood and Carbondale,
our toddler girls wobbled on wet rocks
and played in green bubbles that steamed
at the water's edge. We waited for a pause
in the traffic to jump out and struggle
into our jeans and hiking boots,
wet skin and laughter slowed us down.

In your kitchen we drank honeyed tea
at your dark wooden table, the inheritance
of a child orphaned at eighteen.
Sunlight filtered through cottonwood
leaves and the room was filled with
memory and tomorrow. Your strong
tanned hands cut whole wheat bread
into thick slices that you piled with ripe
avocado, alfalfa sprouts, and tahini.

We talked about our outlaw boyfriends who
became our husbands, who became our
exes. Neither of us ever married again. I lost
track of you but had occasional reports
of your life along the Front Range
and the Western Slope. It didn't sound
easy but you always seemed to manage.

I imagine you now, living in the high
country, probably in an old mining
house. Maybe you are painting again, or
in the evening dusk, your hands
reach out to the potter's wheel
and touch the slippery clay
to make one more pot.

I DROWNED

I drowned that summer
in Cattaraugus Creek,
seventeen and caught
in a whirlpool of foam
and dark shadow sinking
murky gray to thick black to

dazzling light. Chest crushed
with my own breath, no
air, nothing, then caught
by my arm and hauled
out to the stony shore, so
no, not drowned.

Decades later when
that chemical chemo hit,
I gasped a ridiculous *help*
as heavy stones filled
unmovable lungs,

throat narrowed and closing
edge of vision darkening, then
pulled back once more
to sputtering breath.
Again, not drowned.

HALF-FOUND JOHN MUIR POEM #4

How glorious a greeting the sun gives the mountains!
—John Muir

You climbed the High Sierras

in the 1860s, lifted your arms

to *enclose it as in a frame.* Today

I descend this snowy path not far

from home, pause in March sunrise

mirrored off Chugach Range.

The camera's mechanical click, frozen

photo will never carve

image into bone. Homeward,

my ribcage bears this *mighty host*

of mountains, snow-

pack, diamond light, cobalt sky.

RIVER OF MERCY

I.

Merced, River of Our Lady of Mercy,
    flows over gray granite
        with clear light.

Does mercy feel like forgiveness
    of the summer-slow
        stream

or does that clemency clamor
    swift and steep
        falling?

Is mercy the giving green
    of moss-covered
        stone

or the dance of these
    wild grasses
        in the breeze?

II.

The settlers' guide pointed to the valley floor

        and spoke. *Yosemite* was what

            they heard

but just a mistranslation

        of the warning *Yo-hem-a-tee,*

            there are murderers down there.

A year ago two doctors

        stood with solemn sad faces

            and awkward hands, and

in a language of medicine and

        fluorescent scans, said:

            malignancy.

III.

Now plump dogwood blossoms

        offer themselves on tentative branches

            to a soul-blue sky

and a doe with last year's fawns

        feasts on grass, so close I can almost

                touch the velvet of their fur.

IV.

Thank you for Incense Cedar memories

        of winter sweaters

                and dark worn pews,

for Ponderosa Pine in wind

        that whisper like brooms on dawn's

                damp sidewalks,

and for the long-awaited green

        of the Wild Ginger's

                generous heart-shaped leaves.

V.

At night the river sings

      while bass notes

            echo from a thousand frogs.

I wait at the bridge for moonrise.

      Moonlight illuminates

            my skin

and the river threads

      silver in the soft

            gleam.

II

WINTER RAIN

Awake in the middle of the night, I don't know
if I'm six or sixty, but I'm comforted by
the dog's steady snore, the furnace hum,
the wind outside wild like fire

in the forest. Memories skate at the edge
of my mind, stars blur in the dark sky, constellations
undefined. I overheard something a stranger
said; it still echoes like a rock skips

across the silent lake, sound distinct yet
unrecognizable. In the morning, I watch
the pattern of winter rain on window panes.
So much left undone.

HALF-FOUND JOHN MUIR POEM #5

But the darkest scriptures of the mountains are illumined with bright passages of love . . .
—John Muir

You lived as *Nature*
Scribe and Rhapsode,
old man of the Sierras.
I am only an aging woman
who watches her small
slow steps inch uphill.

Arms opened, you held
a *foreground aflame*
with autumn colors.
Talk to me, talk to
me, tell me, and I will

share scrub oak,
fireweed that announces
abundant red, and
cottonwood that fades
yellow like sun that skims
this Chugach range in winter.

SPARGANIA MAGNOLIATA

Double-banded Carpet Moth
trembles on my rug
like a mud smudge
in motion, unable
to fly. I try to encircle
it in my hands
but it is impossible
to capture such
frail darkness.

My fingertips pinch
a wing, and the moth flutters
like the fast beat
of a small bird's heart.
I carry it to the door,
and in the bright sun
drop it to the hard
deck. Dozens more
are still gathered beneath
the shut-off porch light.

Forewings and hind-
wings with scalloped
edges, opened flat
into the outline
of a rough heart, they
were once crawlers
and eaters of fire-
weed. Now, with
slender bodies,

wavy-lined wings
of neutrals and golden
flecks, these moths wait
as if in silent praise.

ON A SUMMER DAY AFTER MY SON AND I
WITNESS A YOUNG MAN'S DROWNING

My grief is heavy

as ripe apples

in the fall

gathered into the circle

of a damp white apron.

His anger is a bit

he can't spit

out. He bites

iron, grinds

the bitter taste.

WHAT IS GATHERED AND WHAT IS LOST

for E.I.

He killed the moose last
fall, shot it twice through
heart and lungs, slid
a knife into soft
belly, spilled stomach,
intestines, the insides out
onto stone and dirt.
Then with warm blood
dried cold on chapped
hands, we packed
down the mountain-
side and across the Matanuska.
Meat weight welded
to our weary backs, sweat
steamed under shoulder
straps, and spruce branches
slapped our faces.
Downed cottonwood stumbled
our swollen feet. Each trip
back up through tundra marsh
and alder thicket more
difficult than the one before.
Dawn to dusk we hauled
our bodies up, the moose
body down.

The metal spoon clangs
my earthenware bowl.
I breathe in
hot broth, bite
into tender meat, the whole
land in every mouthful:
taste willow bud,
muskeg, winter sun.

WALKING HOME

Labrador tea, *Ledum palustris* ssp. *groenlandicum*; heath family:
a low evergreen shrub found in the bogs and on the alpine slopes
of Southcentral Alaska.

She bends to the tundra
        to gather the sharp sweetness
                in a sprig of Labrador tea,

then hikes out from the trail, quiets
        the *whys* and *what ifs* of her mind, quiets
                her too-busy hands. Here, she loses

herself to find herself.
        She wants you to know
                this place of her. She holds

the dark fragrance in her bright palm,
        leaves as small and infinite as stars.

In the distance, the wind
        sighs through the alders.

MORE ACHE THAN THE SEA

Tomorrow waits like a thousand roads

    filled with prisoners

        who march in oblivion.

Today—just the running

    of the clouds

        and these quiet hands.

THE ANCHORAGE JAIL

My son, young inmate,
sprawls along the long table
India ink blue tattoos
accented by orange prison garb;
chin juts forward
looking for a fight
jaw clenched
denying or defying
hard to tell which.
So many scars
up and down
his arms and angry eyes
hold, then hide
so much pain.

We speak through battered
black telephones, cords
spiraled down
with worn metal.
We're joined by shatterproof
glass. He laughs,
cries,
swears
he wants to change.
Mothers trade
in hope and time.

The guard pats my shoulder,
an unexpected kindness,
but I find my way

out the door
alone
across the long parking lot
to my locked car.

EMERGENCY ROOM, WEDNESDAY 4PM

He is patient *26 Hall*,
as if an addict couldn't earn
an actual examination room in the E.R.
Sprawled in a hallway chair next
to the nurses' station, black jeans and hooded
sweatshirt hang on his too-thin frame, two
sizes too big, an overage teen leaning
into a ruined adulthood.

Black ski goggles hang around his neck;
when he puts them on
he looks like a giant fly.
His gray mother perches on a swivel stool
like a dumbed parrot, studies
the flesh-colored linoleum with confetti
pattern of yellow, red, green—all shades
of bodily fluids.

It's a two-hour wait for the doctor, who arrives
like a light breeze in his untouchable
hospital whites, erect from his polished
brown loafers to his perfect
blond haircut. He throws back his head
and laughs when *26 Hall* says he doesn't know
whether to O.D.
or put a bullet in his head.

Two hours more, and they check him
into detox for a three-day
hold. He inches,
like a black beetle, to the end
of the fluorescent-lit hall.

INSIDE OUT

The inchoate chaos of random
> tattoos swarms down his right arm:
grim angels fall from the shoulder,

> the outline of thorned leaf and barbed
wire beginnings encircle
> a lean bicep. Draping his forearm

is a heart like a drupaceous fruit.
> Only the small circle
of his elbow remains

> plain, un-inked like a sorry
sad moon, shining white in a blue sea.

HIS SADNESS IS A LAKE

His sadness is a lake.
If one tear leaks out,
he tells me,
they will
never stop. He leans,
now silent, against the ice

of the passenger window.
The full moon watches through
the falling snow.
I order his Happy
Meal, stare at the bright

red and yellow sign
like it's a star to wish upon.
I roll up the window and hear
the tightness of his grief
sitting in the space

between us.
He is sad because
he is nine. He is sad
because *everything changes.*
I too am still reading

that scripture. The moon
doesn't stay forever, the moon can't
always be seen. The boy turns,
looks out the window. The boy
tries to make himself

invisible. Mommy can't fix
everything. Mommy can't
fix anything. The boy will not cry
tonight. When he is twenty-
three years old he will

remember this night
and cry tears of granite.
Ria, ria rahnka I sing
as my grandmother
sang to me. Crying
is overrated. The moon smiles
as snow drifts on the frozen lake.

THESE MOUNTAINS ARE
LONG-EXTINCT VOLCANOES

The ground below shifts shadow and light, a bewilderment
of late-fall colors: rust, sand, gray. In a four-seater Cessna
we fly over the Talkeetna range, over ground we knew
long ago. We circle Billy Mountain—so close, too close.
I have to look away.

To the west a sorrow of unnamed mountains marches north in ragged
unison, dusted with pure shimmer of a blessing of snow.
Incandescence. At this distance, clarity realized
in the diamond braid of the Nelchina River. Once, sea life
swam these mountains. Ammonite fossils remain
along the riverbed, along the slopes.

Once, we walked the cold creeks, washed ourselves half-clean
after weeks in the tundra. The pilot follows the river. Today
is my son's thirtieth birthday. He says: *You're twice as old
as I am now.* I think: *You are the age I was when you were born.*
Does this have meaning? I was never good at math
and these heights are dizzying.

Remember hot chocolate that tastes of camp smoke?
Fresh-caught arctic char and the greasy sweetness
of Oreos that we packed in? This wasn't before the battles,
but before a divorce which left you stranded on alternating
shores of an unnavigable river.

How could you feel abandoned when we fought over you
at least once a week? The pilot banks south, over lake-studded
lowlands, hidden swamps, erupted peaks, volcanic edifice.
I want this trip to bring back
some remembered joy.
Maybe from this distance, we'll be able to see it.

NEAR POWER CREEK: AFTER A MARRIAGE

In a borrowed red Dodge
  with windshield cracked
I travel alone,
  every mile
wishing away a flat tire.
  The ocean and mountains
of Cordova dissolve,
  replaced by river delta expanse.

   Nearly twenty years I stayed
 with a man who could spot betrayal
   in forgotten condiments
 and spoiled vegetables
   but was blind to the imprint
 his sharp fist left
   upon our living
 room wall.

Fifty empty miles
  of dirt road and at the end:
a rusted cantilevered bridge
  crosses the Copper River;

the simple road disappears

       into a deserted past.

Earthquake and flood splintered

       two bridge spans askew;

18,000 cubic feet of concrete, 5 million

       pounds of steel,

this 1910 celebrated glory

       now cobbled together with sheetmetal.

Once, he sliced

the breakfast bread

       with careless precision

through the forgiving grain,

       while he watched me and made

soft promises with the knife.

The bridge cries

       like a kettledrum

as the pickup rumbles across.

       Child's Glacier and the riotous river

overpower the vacancy.

       The river slides in loud silence back

to tomorrow.

He was unmovable;
me: unable to move.
I can't tell the shame
of my staying so long.

In the distance,
　　the glacier calves:
shotgun boom of ice as it separates
　　and splashes house-sized bergs
into the river, birthing
　　a two-foot wake.
I listen to the sound of the water,
　　the echo of ice letting go.

LOOKING OUT THE WINDOW
ON A WINTER MORNING

Snow breathes in hushed layers,
      blurs with sleep
            garden stones, bare lilacs.
Each flake singular, born of water,
      cloud, nothingness, merges
            to unveil a baptism of light, an indigo
      eulogy of shadow.
In splintered dawn the land sighs:
      downdraft of the owl's white wings.

STILL

In the half-lit dawn
of an autumn morning
my mother stands at her kitchen
counter, prepares my breakfast.
She is seventy-six.
I am fifty-six and visiting her.
She has dipped each peach

into boiling water. She removes
the furred skin skillfully.
In a distilled silence
she holds the slick globe
of juice in her hand, slices bite-
sized wedges. Thick nectar runs

through her fingers.
At our table she places
the glass bowl filled
with sweet ripeness.
Who else will ever
care for me like this?

ANNIVERSARY: MY PARENTS' MARRIAGE

Together they laugh
at the breakfast bar, toast
with glasses of soda,
celebrate the beginning,
their first date, sixty-
one years ago today.

He remembers the time and day
like it's a pocket watch
fastened close to him
with a fine chain.

She remembers the place,
the taste of salt, the sweet sip
of water, how it all left
a new fullness on her tongue.

She gives her weight
to the shovel, but it sinks
so little into the garden clay.
She is smaller now, thinner,
a slow fading away.

He walks his daily
two miles with a lean
and a shuffle
as if he is anchored
to the earth.

Watching him
she already carries
the weight
of his absence.

REDPOLLS IN WINTER

In the thicket, birds flit from branch
        to branch, blush of pinkish breast nestled
in mottled gray-brown feathers, red
        plumage atop their heads,
                puffs of soft color in the gray world.

Small redpolls dust birch limbs,
        hop and bob on snowdrifts below.
This is their daily work:
        knock catkins from branches,
                gather seeds from snow.

The birds rise like applause,
        drift back downward in zigs and zags:
falling autumn leaves,
        cascading acrobats
                tumbling in little dances of splendor.

Snow falls in clumps with seed shells,
        a soft *cluff* sound
on the mounds below.
        So much quiet in all this motion,
                this secret prayer of joy.

III

MYTHOGRAPHY OF THE WOLF'S SORROW
OR AN ALTERNATIVE RENDERING OF
THE ROMULUS AND REMUS LEGEND

I. THE WOLF SPEAKS

I found them naked
cold just the two
furless and frail pale
spindle-limbed babes
their tight red fists grasping
nothing   I lay down
beside them suckled
them like my own

the shepherd took them
as if my own pups
weren't sacrifice
enough even though
I had promised in the night sky
to her wide calm
paleness raised my face

to her face
and cried *take care
of mine and I'll care
for yours*

2. THE SOLDIER SPEAKS

I rough-carried them away,
away from their mother, away
from their home, a newborn
under each arm, just a loaf or a log.

At the shore, my thick hands
trembled like sedges in an uneasy breeze.
Their cloudy infant-blue eyes looked past me
to uncertain futures, looked through me to sky.

Will their downy black hair coarsen,
their heads near small as my fist
grow man-sized, strong-jawed? Will
flexible bones harden toward tomorrow?

Hero or killer? History will appoint
its own standing. I didn't put them in clay
jars deserted by the front door. At least
now they have a beggar's chance.

All lives are held in the hand
of fate. I sent them downriver
in a rough basket. They float homeless,
helpless, hapless. May the gods protect them.

3. THE INFANT TWINS SPEAK

Together we breathed
our first word: *Mother*—
a song of sweet figs on lips,
rumble of opal oceans deep
in the chest, growl
of need in back
of the throat—
but then we were left
only with the burnt aftertaste
of tannined leaves.

4. THE SHEPHERD'S WIFE SPEAKS

The old man brought
them home: puny, puling,
appallingly small,
troublesome two;
I could have done without
either, much less the both.

And the way that wolf
paced, paused, pawed
the woods at night
like she was hungry
for them. Never
trusted any of them.

5. THE WOLF AGAIN SPEAKS

I remember scent of sea
of source   of salt and iron
their breath   all sweet-milk
and mewling green
of spring-born grass

I carried them like a sonnet
like a song in my mouth   now
my heart is a flat river rock or
the birch tree struck
by lightning   bereaved
of all leaves

raven ruffles his feathers
and laughs at death   a mother
would give her life
for her young   but it's a trade
no one   not even god
will take

6. THE MOON SPEAKS

I see her nights
that I'm out
watching.
Each of us
alone.
Her howls echo
in the dark.
She addresses
her plea
as if I

can give
redress
like she
is the injured
plaintiff. I'm

not judge nor
jury here
I'm only
the moon.

I rule tides
I'm keeper of
the night skies
but I
can't heal
an injured
heart. What
do I know
of sorrow?
I'm only
the moon.

TRINITY

Into the slim stalk

    of swirled green glass—

        mouth, an emerald ripple—

three narrow upright petals,

    with three large purple falls;

        each stem breathes a wild iris.

My hands name them:

    Mother, daughter, son.

        Earth, sky, heaven.

TOSCA, ACT V

Tosca never knew the words but found them with her hands
in the night. She is not the same person. She is never the same
person. She hears loss howl like cemetery dogs. She cannot
protect with words, but when she talks to you, she says, *quiet,*
and night knows beauty. *quiet.* And you argue with her, but
her song lives now within you.

HERE THE PROMISE

Here the promise of sky
is more blue than ocean
deep but mountains have no
forgiveness at timberline
and the road winds narrow
and dusty. *Warning: Falling
Rocks*. Drop-offs steep

pull at worn tires. I'm lost
but keep traveling in
this near-exhausted Dodge,
past familiar small towns
that I've never seen
before. I don't know
where I'm headed

or why. This journey must
be its own answer, its own
call. So I shift down
to second gear and edge
uphill in search of the next
rise and a further view.

ONLY WINTER

February is bitter, with only winter
        in its past, winter in its future. I stand
in the church line, my shoes iced
        and damp, the metal sky heavy
inside my head. What do I say
        to the dead boy's ever-absent mother when
I'm trapped in my own storm?

Her face is February, time-bruised and over-
        used but I can see remnants of spring. She
who I knew as a child is a beautiful ruin
        of a woman who still moves her hands
like she is a princess removing a soft veil, still
        watches me with fox-like shyness
and slyness; my next move dictates her change.

I find no comfort in the stadium church
        with hard pews and blustery pastor. Red-faced
young men in stiff shirts and dress pants
        observe from the corners of their eyes
the hurricane force of change. Outside, sleet falls
        at a slant. The streetlight holds its dim haze
and illuminates nothing but the icy rain.

REINCARNATE

Katya moves her cool white hands
trailing winter sunlight
from pale fingertips.
Wrists and palms mimic
her never-known
great-grandmother Mabel,
Mabel as she dried
her hands at her kitchen sink.
Blood tells its secret path
and the body holds
what it never held.

Saldon tells me, "We believe
clear light passes
from one generation
to the next." I don't know
if she means we teach
our children or if this occurs
on a molecular level,
some corpuscular theory
of DNA. I lean in closer,

but she has nothing more

to say. We sip our tea while snow

shimmers across the rough bones

of the mountains.

I BOW

I bow in the monasteries of Drepung and Samye,
offer my Chinese yuan,
follow Tibetan pilgrims.

I cry before the Buddha of Compassion,
the Medicine Buddha who heals,
the Buddha of Loving-Kindness.

Half a world from home and my sorrows are still with me.

KASHIN-BECK DISEASE IS ENDEMIC TO TIBET

Her voice wings like the green
> warbler hops from branch
to higher branch in the alpine
> scrub. She sings in a language
I barely know, the melody bittersweet.
> I sit on the crumbling concrete
wall of the school's courtyard,
> watch her walk like a wise
child in a funeral march.

> Only three feet nine inches tall
and twenty years old, Rinjee
> has already outlived
all expectations. I open my arms,
> feel her distended chest against
my body. She leans into me like a heavy
> toddler, like a building collapsing.
Next to us the little birds dance
> on the fallen concrete remains.

WHO WILL SPEAK OF LHASA?

Tibet, 2011

Even now, distanced
by months and miles,
my words are deadened
by the hollow beat of black boots
on concrete, the slap
of hands on wooden stocks

of semi-automatic rifles.
Juniper still burns sweet
in five-foot stone incense burners
in the public square. Smoke
fills the sky, and my eyes sting.
Soldiers demand the papers

of a young nun in orange robes
and rosewood mala beads,
her shaved head exposed
to cold wind. Nomads
prostrate across the length
of the square, rough wood blocks

tied to their palms. Old and young,
they slide their bodies flat
onto the cobblestone, until
they are pulled aside and loaded
into the back of an olive-green truck

that rumbles away. I avoid
the soldiers' eyes, their faces—
masks trained for no expression.
Their eyes watch
everything but see no one.

You can not tell this.

In the east,
a hundred small and terrible fires
burn, silent and invisible.

FAITH

Most of the sangha blamed me for my loss of faith, for my non-attendance. When I finally showed up one day, they knew I didn't understand anything anymore. They instructed me when I forgot the words, forgot the gestures. But they didn't know me. One woman pulled me aside to whisper of the monk's secret sins, his lasciviousness, his lies. But I thought: he is just a man in love. Look at his wood carvings. His own hands made those. His hands that are old but still strong. Still reaching. Look: perfect longing. Perfect trust. That carving of him, arms open, leaping from a cliff to meet his love. He has been working on this for years.

ALL THINGS ARE TRANSIENT

B&W photograph, 1924

I became like my grandmother,
            young in that photograph,
but the image fading, black
            and white into light.

She stands at a station,
            in transit, no
arrival, no departure,
            no destination.

Simply traveling.
            If she were to speak, surely
she would stammer,
            unsure, her small smile

vanish, her expression then
            stunned. I watch
as the lightness,
            which began

in her chest,

      spreads until she

looks pure light,

      transparent.

DR. ANDERSON CALLED AND
THE NEWS ISN'T GOOD

I heard it. That sound
loud like the other shoe
dropping, like that fine
china heirloom cup slipped
from my damp hand
and clattered, shattered
on cold wood. All my
fault. I turn

towards the window to see
that terrible bounce of bird
thrown back from glass,
fall to the ground, a thick
black mass. I look down
and see him on his side,
right wing half-lifted, twitches
as life leaves his body. His wings

are black as winter's night;
white spots glow like snow
illuminated by moon, like stars

falling fill darkness. Soft
belly feathers tremble
with breath, spot of blood-
red feathers crown
dark head. He is
beautiful. Motionless.

I extract *Guide to the Birds
of Alaska* from my bookshelf. Let
me identify him, know
him before I bury
him. As if science could
change reality, as if naming
could save and re-make. A half-
hour passes and I put
my coat on to go

dig a small grave
on this sunny autumn
day full of golden falling.
But now, he's perched
on the ground, upright,

but dazed. An hour
later, he's gone, and only
a wisp of feather remains,
a soft white fluttering.

THIS BODY IS BAGGAGE I'M NOT YET
READY TO LEAVE BEHIND

Raven, crow's old uncle, shanties
on the week-old dirty snowpile, casts
a knowing look, undiscernible
as pity or dislike. *Another nail
in the coffin*. We speak grief in layers
of deepest blue, in riven glaciers

calved into endless night seas. Remember
the promise of spring? Bitter-
sweet birch leaves and the gold beacon
of forsythia flame? It has failed us;
time fractured and fallen. The granite moon
abandons day's light. We are sundered

and shattered; unsurrendered, but frayed
as smoke in the midnight sky.

IV

THIS IS A RAGING WIND

This is a raging wind
that tastes like aluminum foil,
smells like rusty iron,
feels like electricity through my hands.
It whines like mosquitoes in my ears.
It is a ghost, pale and bald.
I can smell the dying hair.

This is a silent spider,
hidden and deadly.
There are small areas of residual
hyper-metabolic uptake in the pelvis.
Spiders used to not frighten me.

Dr. Hope at Providence
Hospital says, *Primum non nocere.*
I say suffering is the quickest way
to learn gratitude.
The sun smiles, a muted haze, behind
clouds that linger in the western sky.

SINCE JUNE

I thought I saw you today

        but you've been gone

    since June.   I stood in the sanctuary

          of the Church of a Thousand Logs, read,

               as your family had asked, Hunt's

    "Abou Ben Adhem."   I forgot

                     myself, followed the turn

       of the words. I forgot my spring-green

          and pale-pink cancer scarf

tight-wrapped around my head.

                 Moonfaced, moonstruck, bemoaning,

             beholding. Mooning over my lost self.

They treated me with the tenderness

       reserved for the already dead.

From the streetlight, the raven talks to me

        with his dark guttural *gaalk, gaalk,*

             lifts his wings skyward

         to the dim winter sun   glides

      south towards the river,

           sound swallowed now

a bubble in his closed throat.

WALK ON WATER

Made dizzy by endless
clear water, lightning-
cracks of white,
dotted with black
pebbles scattered
through, I stand
on the frozen lake.

This inverse universe
is at my feet. No wonder
I wonder, feel that I will fall
in an endless falling through
time and dark space as deep
as night blue. I don't
believe in magic
stability. There is no safety,
no permanent solidarity

of molecules. Each
step is unexpected.
I want to call out to you—
my world, my love, my life—

I haven't breathed
every breath. I still need
to capture fog
in a jar, read the trunks

of trees with my blind
inelegant fingertips.
I want to stand at the edge
of this abyss, look

down into the frozen
lake and make myself
look past dizziness. I want
to see it all.

HALF-FOUND JOHN MUIR POEM #1

Now came the solemn, silent evening.
—John Muir

Now comes *silent,*

    solemn evening

to Talkeetna Mountains

    shattered and scattered

against northern sky.

I watch clouds wing

    crimson across

ragged peaks

    kindled by

the setting sun.

Then comes

    darkness and the stars

and spruce branches

    that whisper over me

as I sleep towards dawn.

GE(NE)OLOGY

At dawn, sheltered from wind
and snow, my daughter reads
Greek myths to me while I curl
in the warmth of my sleeping
bag. In the tent, my eyes closed,
I fall through layers of limestone
and conglomerate. The dark
of my eyelids: filled
with endless rocks patterned

by bivalve fossils, hundreds
in each stone, and I can still
smell herbal Artemisia waft
through the tundra where we
walked all yesterday. Her
grown-competent hands
prepare our meal. I let her
take care of me. Later, she

rests while I read John Muir
out loud. When I look over,
her eyelashes lie thick
on sunny cheeks, somehow

unchanged after all this time,

and I remember all those bedtime

stories, all those quiet moments

when I was first

a mother.

HALF-FOUND JOHN MUIR POEM #2

After lying loose and lost . . . , I made a sunrise fire.
—John Muir

I came to the Talkeetnas

        to rest myself

in silence. *Never*

           was mountain more home.

Fog and snow roll

        in with night. Ice

pelts the tent. When the sun rises,

          cold and dark melt *back*

into the immeasurable

          blue. All things now *warm*

and awaken. Look:

        this day.

ON A SUMMER DAY

The high meadows above the lake grow

       fireweed aflame in fuchsia, white medicinal yarrow,

       and ever-invasive, always-thriving purple

       vetch. Graveyard mounds of vetch.

       In our small-town paper I see his photo: young, smiling.

The thrum of mosquitoes in the heat

       of a heavy day, leafy cottonwood—all obscure my view.

       I hear a shout and one word: Police. Then nothing.

       Nothing. The lapping sound of water on shore.

       Does it matter how he died? Or only that he is dead?

I look at my son; we look across the calm

       lake, muddy bank with murky turquoise

       water, gray that hides blue, gray that hides

       green, cold sheen of sun across the slight waves.

       His family was nearby on the bank watching.

Silence. I see nothing, only my dog shaking

       wet fur that curls and swirls against his strong

       body. My son thinks there's trouble, but then

       sees a head pop out of the water near a fallen tree.

       James. Twenty-two years old.

More silence. We leave. Everything must be fine. I insist.

       I know, because it's quiet. On the way

       home we are passed by the loud wails

of ambulances. Six, seven vehicles counted.

State troopers responded to CPR in progress. He was later
pronounced dead.

How do I mourn for someone I didn't know? There is no way
to right this. There is no right way. I walk the meadows
above the lake to feel
the hot sun on my face. I watch the solitary
robin watch me from the farm fencepost.

I look up at an eagle, wings spread wide open, circling
above the lake. The lake only reflects the hard
glare of sunlight on its surface; dark.

SUN LIKE A DAFFODIL

I wander not lonely

       but alone

on this *pathless path*,

       a traveler who

hasn't lived or died

       enough. I carry

the ecstasy of sun, pressed

       against my longing.

A LIGHT IN WINTER

I turn my back to our bonfire, shield
my face from smoke, study
the immense sky. The moon, born
of sun and night, rises above
the snow-covered mountain,
seems to pause,

a goblet lifted in pledge
by fingertip branches
of the bare birch. The moon changes
as it rises. I stand between
worlds of voice and silence, in my own
place of transition. Around the campfire—

three conversations; on the hill
I hear shouts and laughter
of the sledders. I am part of all
this, part of none. When I finally
leave the campfire, the moon
has disappeared behind light clouds.

I drive on the two-lane road,
often so dark even bright
headlights might not
show what lurks in the deep
snow. Moose may wander
out, they don't know

the danger. There are worse
ways to die, but neither
the moose nor I are ready.
Tonight, the snow reflects
some light from the half-
hidden moon.

HALF-FOUND JOHN MUIR POEM #3

In so wild and so beautiful a region . . . every sight and
sound inspiring, leading one far out of himself . . .
—John Muir

Mr. Muir, John seems too informal although

I've carried your book for months

(*what a fine traveling companion it proved*

to be), *The Mountains of California*, muted gray-

green (like my moss-heathered tundra) cover

that contains your words, (your *Cassiope*, your *redemption*

of the coldest solitude) presses against

my back, insisting, persisting whenever

it is tucked in my pack. We both have known hard magic

of these wild (*every feature more rigidly*

alpine) places where we write of (our own) limitless

blue sky encircled by peaks *clothed with light*. In

the mountains of Alaska, with your book, I wait

for (not) inspiration but

ice cascade, landslide, avalanche.

REMISSION

Six months ago I was afraid if I moved my hand too quickly
        the sky
might crack open, might fall apart. Now, driving home, the sky extends
        endlessly blue,

blue of Alaska's Mendenhall Glacier, blue of the high holy lakes
        of the Himalayas, and
against the blue are scattered strata clouds, stretched long like lovers' tangled
        sheets, scratched

like soft chalk marks on a dark board, and slices of bright sunlight layer gold
        between sky and
cloud, and the snow on the mountain pretends purple against gray granite
        all so clear

it seems I can reach across into valleys, stroke the spruce. I almost pull over
        but then the snow
blows off the ridgeline and blurs into the clouds until there is no end
        of mountain, no beginning of sky.

HALF-FOUND LI SHANG-YIN POEM

When will I be home?... Tonight on the stormy mountain.
—Li Shang-yin

When will I be home?

    In the mountains,

in the rainy night

    of autumn. When wild

wind rushes high

    through branches letting go

of leaves too golden

    to hold. When rain

blows sideways to christen

    my face dew-like. When

the campfire smolders

    and smoke nests

in my hair. I wait

    for silence, only

for the turning of the earth.

TOMORROW IS A WHITE FLAG

Yesterday flutters like clean laundry:
the sound of sheets on a Monday
morning clothesline—all flap
and slap, work-shirts with scent
of sky, and sweet-as-green-grass socks
alchemized into cardboard.
On Wheelock Street the Miskys,
the Heintzes, and the Joyces all
hung out clean wet clothes in spring.

Tomorrow is yesterday's
laundry and the past is just
a white flag. I thought Oxydol
laundry soap must have a doll
inside the box, dressed in a white
and green dress, just like the detergent
flakes. That name was a promise
to the four-year-old Jules. But autumn
always arrives. The dead rope
of hope curls on the cold garage
floor, frozen into an unmovable mound.
I give up.

The white flag flies near
the horizon; forgiving flags
should fly more often. I believe
in the certainty of an afterlife:
the more things change, the more
they stay the same. The freezing
shirts grow restless, fold inward
on themselves, while against

the setting sun, sheets ripple
like Northern Lights faded
to wisps of white.

UNRAVEL

She thought she could unravel the sound

of the river, hear the water whisper an answer,

was it *love* or *loss*? Rocks might declaim

stable or *stumble* to her searching

feet. Distant stars spill cold light, dispel

the implied obligation of all those

wishes. There is loneliness in not knowing, in being

unable to read the secret

of open skies or to catch

the quiet prayer in the water's reply.

SKY BURIAL

Talkeetna Mountains, Alaska

What better place to write
    a death poem than here
        at the top of the world?

Here, where mountains hold
    the child-blue sky with
        its whisper of clouds.

Here, where the trail weaves through
    a rejoicing of alpine wildflowers—
        saxifrage, cinquefoil, moss heather.

Bury me to the sky.
    Let my bones be alms
        for the birds.

NOTES

"Half-Found John Muir Poem" #4, #5, #1, #2, and #3: These poems were inspired by John Muir's writing in *Essential Muir*, ed. Fred D. White (Berkeley, Calif.: Heyday Books, 2006), 37–54. The italicized words within each poem are Muir's own words, as found in his original writings, with two exceptions: in Poem #5, "Nature Scribe and Rhapsode" is the title of Part Three of *Essential Muir*; and in Poem #2, the original "warming and awakening" has been changed to "warm and awake." The poems are numbered in the order in which they were written and were intentionally placed in the order in which they appear here.

"Reincarnate": Saldon is the name of a Tibetan woman; most Tibetan names are gender neutral.

"I Bow": Drepung and Samye are major monasteries in the Tibet Autonomous Region (TAR). Drepung was once the largest monastery in Tibet, with as many as ten thousand monks. The current population is difficult to determine, with estimates varying between two hundred and six hundred monks. Samye was the first Buddhist monastery in Tibet, and thus is the region's oldest, dating to the eighth century.

"Kashin-Beck Disease Is Endemic to Tibet": Kashin-Beck or "big bone" disease is a chronic joint disorder that affects growth and causes osteoarthritis. It is suspected to be caused by environmental factors.

"Sun like a Daffodil": This poem owes its inspiration to Ilya Kaminsky's line "and I grow frightened that I haven't lived, died, not enough . . . ," from "Musica Humana," in *Dancing in Odessa* (Dorset, Vt.: Tupelo Press, 2004), 17. The poem was also influenced by William Wordsworth's "The Daffodils."

"Half-Found Li Shang-yin Poem": This poem was inspired by Li Shang-yin's poem "When Will I Be Home?," translated by Kenneth Rexroth in *One Hundred More Poems from the Chinese: Love and the Turning Year* (New York: New Directions, 1976), 77. The italicized words are from the original poem.

"Unravel": This poem was inspired by the line "She thought she could unravel the sounds the river made" in Marilynne Robinson's novel *Lila* (New York: Farrar, Straus and Giroux, 2014), 59.

"Sky Burial": The title of this poem refers to the Tibetan funeral practice of leaving the bodies of the dead at high altitudes to feed the wild animals and birds.

ACKNOWLEDGMENTS

Grateful acknowledgments are made to the editors of those publications in which the following poems, or earlier versions, originally appeared.

Bluestem: "Reincarnate"
Cirque: "Near Power Creek: After a Marriage" and "The Anchorage Jail"
Lummux: "Emergency Room, Wednesday 4pm" and "Not a Fairy-Tale Ending"
Northern Cardinal Review: "Looking out the Window on a Winter Morning" and "Redpolls in Winter"
Passager: "His Sadness Is a Lake"
Pilgrimage: "What Is Gathered and What Is Lost"
Poetry Quarterly: "Kashin-Beck Disease Is Endemic to Tibet"
Potomac Review: "Tosca Lived a Good Life"
Riding Light: "All Things Are Transient" and "These Mountains Are Long-Extinct Volcanoes"
Split Rock Review: "Ge(ne)ology"
Sugar Mule: "Walking Home" and "*Spargania magnoliata*"

I am forever grateful to Peggy Shumaker, Alaska Literary Series Editor, for saying yes to this book and believing in its possibility. I am also grateful to the board and all the staff of the University of Alaska Press who shepherded the manuscript through the acquisition and publication process; special thanks to James Englehardt, Amy Simpson, and Krista West. Heartfelt thanks also to manuscript reviewers Holly J. Hughes and Jill McCabe Johnson and copy editor Jane Lyle.

This book would never have come into being if it were not for all the people at the MFA program of Antioch University, Los Angeles. Immense thanks to mentors Jenny Factor, Carol Potter, Jim Daniels, and Richard Garcia; the Blue Spruce cohort; and my fellow poets. Being a part of Antioch's community of writers has taught me much about working together with kindness and toward social justice.

I would also like to thank my friends in Tibet, especially Tenzin, who always welcomed me as if I were one of the family. I deeply appreciate all that Tenzin and her father have shared with me; their perspective has changed my poetry and me.

Last, and most of all, I'd like to thank my family: my parents, Jim and Michele Hungiville; my brother, Michael Hungiville; and my children, Eowyn LeMay Ivey and Forrest LeMay. Without the love and support of my family, this book would never have been completed. This book is also for my granddaughters, Grace and Aurora Ivey, and in memory of my grandmother, Mabel Swanson Gallagher, who found her way into more than one poem.